A Little Princess

Retold from the Frances Hodgson Burnett original by Tania Zamorsky

Illustrated by Lucy Corvino

STERLING CHILDREN'S BOOKS
New York

STERLING CHILDREN'S BOOKS
New York

An Imprint of Sterling Publishing Co., Inc.
1166 Avenue of the Americas
New York, NY 10036

ISBN 978-1-4027-9465-0

Library of Congress Cataloging-in-Publication Data

Zamorsky, Tania.
A little princess / abridged by Tania Zamorsky; illustrated by Lucy Corvino; retold from the Frances Hodgson Burnett original.
p. cm.—(Classic starts)
Summary: An abridged version of the tale of Sara Crewe, a pupil at Miss Minchin's London school, who is left in poverty when her father dies but is later rescued by a mysterious benefactor.
ISBN 1-4027-1275-8
[1. Boarding schools—Fiction. 2. Schools—Fiction. 3. Orphans—Fiction. 4. London (England)—Social life and customs—19th century—Fiction.] I. Corvino, Lucy, ill. II. Burnett, Frances Hodgson, 1849-1924. Little princess. III. Title. IV. Series.
PZ7.Z25457Li 2004

2004013450

Distributed in Canada by Sterling Publishing Co., Inc.
c/o Canadian Manda Group, 664 Annette Street
Toronto, Ontario M6S 2C8, Canada
Distributed in the United Kingdom by GMC Distribution Services
Castle Place, 166 High Street, Lewes, East Sussex BN7 1XU, England
Distributed in Australia by NewSouth Books
University of New South Wales, Sydney, NSW 2052, Australia

For information about custom editions, special sales, and premium and corporate purchases, please contact Sterling Special Sales at 800-805-5489 or specialsales@sterlingpublishing.com.

Manufactured in China

Lot#:
4 6 8 10 9 7 5 3
06/19

sterlingpublishing.com

Design by Renato Stanisic
Cover illustration by Lucy Corvino

CONTENTS

CHAPTER 1

Sara

Not terribly long ago, on a dark winter's day, a little girl sat in a coach with her father and stared out the windows at the broad, fog-covered streets of London. It seemed to her like only yesterday that they had been strolling the sunny streets of India. But, of course, it hadn't been yesterday. They had taken a long sea voyage, and now they were here in this new and strange place.

Sara was only seven, but felt very much older, as though she had lived a long, long time.

"Papa," she said, as the coach started to slow down. "Papa?"

Captain Crewe looked down at his daughter. "Yes, my Little Missus?"

Captain Crewe was a boyish, happy-go-lucky sort of man with a post in the British army in India. "Little Missus" was his pet name for her because she seemed to be so old-fashioned and wise for her age. Sara loved it when he called her that.

"Are we there yet?" she whispered. The driver steered the coach through tall iron gates and into a cobblestone square.

"Yes, Sara, we are finally here." Although he tried to hide his sadness, Sara knew that he wished they hadn't arrived.

For a long time now, he had been preparing her for "here"—the boarding school that was to be her new home. Because the climate of India was bad for children—either blazing hot, or cold and wet during the monsoons—they were generally sent away to England. She had seen other children go, and sometimes felt excited about leaving on such an adventure herself, but was sad and scared at the thought of parting from her father.

"It will only be for a little while," her papa had always said. Everyone would be nice to her there, and he would send her plenty of books that she would devour. Before she knew it, she would be grown up and smart enough to come back to India and take care of him.

Sara liked the thought of that. Since her mother had died when Sara was born, only the two of them were left, to take care of each other. For that reason only, she decided she would go.

"Well," she said, teasing him, "if I have plenty of books, I guess I shall be all right."

Her father laughed and kissed her. He wasn't sure *he* would be all right, though, without his sprightly little companion Sara, but he knew he must keep that a secret for her sake.

The driver let them out in front of a big brick building that seemed fussy and old, but at the same time, stiff and cold. An engraved brass plate on the front door read:

MISS MINCHIN
Select Boarding School for Young Ladies

They pulled open the heavy door and went inside.

The first thing Sara thought of when Miss Minchin entered the room was that she, too, was fussy and old, but somehow also stiff and cold.

Miss Minchin smiled a fake and fishy smile.

"It will be a great honor to take care of such a *clever* and *beautiful* child, Captain Crewe," she flattered Sara.

Sara thought about Miss Minchin's words. She supposed that she was clever for her age—

she had often heard people say so to her papa—Miss Minchin was right about that. However, although mistaken, Sara was thinking that she was not beautiful at all. "I am the skinniest, ugliest girl in the world," she thought. "Miss Minchin is a big storyteller."

Later she would learn that Miss Minchin said the same things to each parent who brought a child to her school.

Sara listened while her papa and Miss Minchin talked. Sara was to be given anything she asked for, they agreed, and Captain Crewe's business manager, of the firm Barrow and Skipworth, would pay all her bills.

At the school, she was to have a pretty bedroom and sitting room of her own, toys, and treats to eat, along with a pony and carriage. To replace her Indian nanny, her *ayah* who was so devoted to her, she would even have her own French maid—Mariette. Another little girl might be spoiled by such pampering, Captain Crewe said, but not his Sara.

And for a friend while her papa was away, Sara would have a special doll she had named Emily. Emily was one of the gifts Captain Crewe and Sara had bought during the previous day's shopping. He had also bought her dresses and hats trimmed with feathers and fur, tiny gloves, scarves, and many pairs of silk stockings. The saleswomen had whispered to each other that Sara must be the daughter of an Indian prince, or *rajah*.

But of all the new things, Emily was Sara's favorite. With her bright blue eyes and shiny hair, and the matching clothes they had picked out together, the doll looked almost human—like Sara's little sister. Best of all, she seemed to really listen when Sara talked, which was unusual for a doll. After seeing hundreds of dolls that day, Sara knew Emily the minute she saw her in the window. It was like recognizing an old friend.

The evening before he was to return to India, Captain Crewe took Sara to Miss Minchin's to spend her first night alone. As they said good-bye, Sara sat on her father's lap and stared at him. She seemed afraid to even blink, lest she lose sight of him for one second.

"Are you trying to learn me by heart?" he asked.

"No," she answered. "I already know you by heart. You are *inside* my heart." And, closing her eyes only then, she hugged him as if she would never let go.

After her father left, Sara went to her room and closed the door. Hours went by without a peep to be heard from inside. Miss Minchin's fat and frumpy sister, Miss Amelia, didn't know what to make of it.

"Well, at least she isn't kicking and screaming

like some of them do," Miss Minchin said tartly.

Miss Amelia had unpacked Sara's things earlier, and hadn't known what to make of them, either. Although Miss Amelia was more sweet-natured than her sister, it was sometimes hard to tell, since she was afraid to disobey Miss Minchin.

"They are ridiculous," Miss Minchin said. "That child has been spoiled as if she were a little princess!"

Miss Amelia nodded in agreement.

"Still," Miss Minchin added, "I do believe that Sara will make us look good at the head of the line when we take the girls to church on Sunday." Miss Minchin was very worried about how she looked to the rest of the world. She hoped that Sara would be a model pupil, in more ways than one.

Upstairs, Sara and Emily sat at the window, still staring at the empty street corner where

Captain Crewe's coach had vanished from sight. He had waved to them out the back window as if he could not bear to say good-bye.

Sara didn't know if she would be able to bear it, either.

The next morning while dressing for her first day of school, Sara sighed to her doll, "Oh Emily, I wish you could go to class with me."

Mariette, who was helping Sara get ready, looked at her as if she were crazy for talking to a doll.

"What are you staring at?" Sara asked in her fluent French, shrugging. "I'll have you know, dolls lead secret lives. They can walk and talk, but," she paused, "will only do so when nobody is watching."

"Why?" Mariette asked her, also in French.

"Well, if people knew what dolls could do," Sara replied, "they would make them do their chores!"

"I know I would," Mariette said. How funny Sara was, she thought next. Always saying "please" and "thank you," Sara had the air of a perfect little princess.

When Sara walked into the classroom, everyone turned to gaze. Lavinia Herbert, who was thirteen, was staring especially hard. Lottie Legh was looking at her cross-eyed, but then, she was only four.

"For heaven's sake," Lavinia whispered to her friend Jessie, "look at what the new girl is wearing. Frills and more frills, and more frills still!"

"She has silk stockings on!" Jessie whispered back. "And look at her tiny feet!"

"Please," sniffed Lavinia. "Even enormous feet look tiny when shoved into silk stockings! I don't think she is pretty at all—she looks rather odd."

Jessie nodded. She was afraid of Lavinia. But when Lavinia wasn't looking, Jessie stole another glance across the room in secret. She wasn't sure if Sara was pretty, either, but there was something about Sara that made her want to look again. Perhaps it was her tall, slim build, or her very black, curled-up hair. Or maybe it was her uncommon gray-green eyes that looked at you with a strange wisdom far beyond that of a seven-year-old.

Miss Minchin rapped on her desk for silence.

"Young ladies," she called out. "Please stand." The girls rose in their places. "This is Miss Crewe, our new student. She has come to us all the way from *Injah*!"

The girls bowed and Sara curtsied back.

"Let's get started," Miss Minchin said. "Because your papa hired a French maid for you, I believe it is because he wants you to study French."

"Oh Miss Minchin," Sara said, "with all due

respect, I think he hired her because he thought I might like her!"

Miss Minchin's fake fish-smile turned into a displeased frown.

"You are a spoiled little girl!" she snapped. But then, she quickly changed her tone. It wouldn't look good for Sara to complain to her rich father. "All I mean," she corrected herself, "is that things in this life are not always done because you like them."

Sara didn't know what to do. She could not remember a time when she did not speak French. Her mother had been French. Her father had spoken French to her as a baby. And earlier, when she was telling Mariette about Emily's secret life, she had spoken and thought in French as well.

But like everyone else, Sara was a bit afraid of Miss Minchin.

"I—I have never really learned French, but—" she began, trying to explain.

"But nothing!" Miss Minchin said, snapping again in spite of herself. "You will start first-year French class today. The French teacher, Monsieur Dufarge, will be here shortly. Now sit down!"

At the end of the girls' first class, Monsieur Dufarge took Sara to a room off the main hall for a private lesson. He was a nice man, with a curly French mustache. He started slowly and simply, telling Sara the French words for "dog" and "cat." Next he tried to teach her to say "spoon" and "fork."

"I have to try again," Sara thought. "Maybe I can make *him* understand."

And so she did. She looked up into Monsieur Dufarge's kind face and, in a soft and fluent French whisper, explained everything.

Monsieur Dufarge smiled so widely that the ends of his mustache curled up.

He later told Miss Minchin, "Ah, Madame.

"This girl does not need to learn French, she *is* French!"

The other pupils had been listening and, on hearing this, some started giggling.

"She could have told me," Miss Minchin said, glaring at Sara, "instead of making me look like a fool!" It was the beginning of Miss Minchin's uneasy feeling about Sara. Somehow, the little girl almost seemed to see right through her!

CHAPTER 2

Making New Friends

Chubby Ermengarde St. John hadn't laughed when Sara embarrassed Miss Minchin by mistake with her fluent French. There was nothing funny, Ermengarde thought, about how stupid she was compared with this new student. Compared with anyone, really—or so her father always said. Her father was a scholar and expected his daughter to read and understand books he sent her. But it was hopeless, because Ermengarde could not remember what she had just read and was the biggest dunce in the school. She had been studying

French for years, with no success. And her pronunciation was just awful. She was, as the French say, *"stupide!"*

Lost in thought, she did not notice that she was chewing on her pigtails. As her father said, she was always chewing on something. Unfortunately, Miss Minchin did notice.

"Miss St. John!" Miss Minchin burst out. "Stop chewing on your hair!"

Ermengarde was startled and blushed bright red. She noticed Sara watching her, which only made her feel worse. "Wonderful," she thought, "now the new girl thinks I am stupid, too."

Or maybe not. When the lessons were done, Sara came over to her.

"I love your name," Sara said sweetly. "Ermengarde . . ." she pronounced slowly. "It sounds like a name in a storybook."

"Do you think so?" Ermengarde asked. When Sara said it, it did sound kind of royal.

"Hey," Sara said, suddenly. "Would you like to come up and meet Emily?"

"Who is she?" Ermengarde asked.

"Come up to my room and see," Sara said. She held out her hand.

"Is it true that you have a sitting room all to yourself?" Ermengarde asked Sara as they climbed the steps to her room.

"Yes," Sara answered. "My papa got me one. When I make up stories and tell them to Emily, I don't like anyone else to hear me."

Ermengarde gasped. "You speak French—*and* make up stories?"

"Why, anyone can make up stories," Sara said. "You can, too."

Ermengarde didn't believe her, but there was no time to protest. When they got to her closed door, Sara put her finger to her lips.

"Shhh," she whispered, mysteriously. "Let's try to catch her!"

Ermengarde didn't know what Sara was talking about, but it sounded very magical. Sara flung open the door, and Ermengarde peered in, but the only thing she saw was a beautiful doll propped up in a chair by the fireplace.

"That sly one," Sara said, chuckling. "She got back to her seat before we could catch her. They always do!"

Ermengarde did not seem to understand, so Sara told her about the secret lives of dolls.

Ermengarde now looked not only confused, but afraid. What else had a secret life? she wondered. Maybe the furniture, too? She glanced down at her chair with suspicion.

"Don't worry," Sara said. "It's only make-believe. Haven't you ever pretended things?"

"No," Ermengarde admitted.

"Don't worry," Sara said. "It's easy. I'll teach you how."

For the next hour, Ermengarde sat hugging

her knees in delight as Sara taught her the basics of pretending—of telling stories and making up odd things. She couldn't teach her French in one hour, but she taught her more about the secret life of dolls, and about the voyage from India. Finally, she told her about her papa.

At that point, she stopped. Sara's face puckered up and she looked like she might cry.

"Are you all right?" Ermengarde asked.

"Do you love your papa?" Sara asked.

"I hardly ever see him," Ermengarde told Sara. "But I must love him, must I not?"

"I love mine more than anything else in the world," Sara blurted out. "And I miss him *so much*." She looked up and sighed deeply. "But I promised him I would be a strong little soldier, and I shall. I shall!"

Ermengarde, inspired by Sara, had an idea of her own. "Lavinia and Jessie are best friends," she said. "Do you think we could be best friends, too? Even if we had to pretend?"

"Why, I think that's a wonderful idea!" Sara said. "No pretending required!"

~

"Lavinia hates you," Ermengarde informed Sara the next day in the parlor. She looked over her shoulder for fear that Lavinia was listening. "Before you came, she was the smartest and best-dressed girl in the school. Lavinia was *important*."

"But Lavinia has no reason to hate me," Sara said. "She is just jealous. She can still be important—everyone is." Ermengarde blinked at this. "Even me?" she was thinking.

Truth be told, Lavinia was a spiteful young girl and was used to lording it over the other children. Before Sara arrived, Lavinia sat next to Miss Minchin at meals and walked at the head of the line on school outings. But no longer.

Out of fairness, Sara believed that things

happen to people by accident. She thought, "It's not my fault that I always liked school, and have a papa who loves me and gives me nice things."

"At any rate," Sara said firmly, "I don't hate Lavinia."

"You're too nice to hate anyone," Ermengarde said. Sara thought for a moment.

"I try to be nice," Sara confessed. "But how do I know if I really am? After all, it's easy to be nice when your life is easy. If my life was harder, and I went through many trials, maybe I would not be so nice. Maybe I would be nasty!"

Sara and Ermengarde's talk was cut short by a powerful, high-pitched scream. They looked over to see Lavinia standing over Lottie. On Lottie's cheek was a fresh red mark—about the size of Lavinia's right hand. "Speaking of nasty . . ." mumbled Ermengarde.

"She slapped me!" Lottie wailed.

Sara rushed over, making a wall between

Lavinia and Lottie. "What were you thinking?" she shouted at Lavinia. "Lottie is only four. You are nearly thirteen—nine years older!"

"My, how we can add," Lavinia said. She was thinking that she would very much like to slap Sara, too. But instead, she turned up her nose and stormed out of the room.

Even with Lavinia gone, Lottie would not stop crying. Lottie was the baby not only of the school, but also of her family, and had been pampered and humored all her young life. Unlike Sara, Lottie had been spoiled by her pampering. Her mother had died, and the people around her gave her the notion that she could use this fact to get special attention. She never said "please" or "thank you." Whenever she wanted something, she kicked and screamed. And little Lottie had quite a pair of lungs: when she screamed, almost all of London could hear her.

Miss Minchin and Miss Amelia could

certainly hear her. Both of them came running.

"What is going on here?" Miss Minchin demanded. "Lottie, why are you crying?"

"Lavinia slapped her," Ermengarde said.

"I'm sure that's not true," Miss Minchin replied. "Lavinia is a lady."

"Ohhhhhhhhhhh!" Lottie screamed, still kicking. "I don't have a—"

"Poor thing," said Miss Amelia. "What does she need?"

"She needs to be spanked," Miss Minchin said. "That's what!"

At this, Lottie's cries became even louder.

"Miss Minchin," said Sara. "May I try to talk to her? Perhaps it will calm her down."

Miss Minchin nodded curtly.

Sara sat down on the floor beside Lottie. Only instead of talking, Sara just looked at her without saying a word. No one knew what to make of Sara's odd ways.

Lottie didn't know what to think, either. Usually, when she cried, everyone made a big fuss. They begged her to stop, promising her anything she wanted if only she would be quiet. But Sara's behavior was so unusual that Lottie forgot to keep screaming.

"Hello," Sara said when Lottie was finally silent. Lottie sniffled a "Hi" in response.

"Why are you crying?" Sara inquired.

"I don't have a—" Lottie began.

"Go on," Sara said to encourage her.

"I don't have a mama!" Lottie finally blurted out. And, although her lower lip still shook, a miracle happened and she was quiet.

"Is that true?" Sara asked Miss Minchin. Perhaps Lottie was not so lucky after all.

"Yes," said Miss Minchin, plainly. "Lottie's mother died when she was little."

At this, Lottie's face turned bright red. She seemed to be getting ready to kick and scream all over again. But Sara spoke before Lottie could start. "Neither do I," she said.

Lottie blinked. Here was another surprise. Lottie didn't want to stop crying, but now she was confused—it was no use. "Where is she?" she asked.

"She is in heaven," Sara replied. "Well, most of the time . . ."

Lottie's eyes widened. "Where is she the rest of the time?" Lottie asked.

And so Sara told Lottie her ideas about angels. Just like dolls, she explained, they led secret after-lives, at times coming back to earth to watch over the people they loved.

Lottie sat up and looked around. The thought that her mama might be somewhere nearby, watching, made her want to act more like a girl who might be related to an angel.

"Tell me more!" Lottie ordered. Sara's stories were as good as candy.

Sara began to talk, her eyes shining and her cheeks flushed. Many other girls gathered around to listen. They became spellbound by Sara's stories, too. The way she told them made them seem almost real.

Sara's voice was dreamy as she described heaven. "There are fields of flowers," she imagined. "The little children run and gather armfuls of them, and laugh, and make long lily necklaces. And there are fairies everywhere, just floating."

"I want to float with the fairies," Lottie declared, "'cause I haven't got any mama down here."

"I will be your mama." Sara knew just what to say. "We'll pretend that you are my adopted little girl. And Emily will be your sister."

When Lottie smiled, her face turned into one big dimple.

"Will she?" asked the big dimple. "Really?"

"Yes," Sara said, jumping to her feet. "Let's go and tell her!"

Lottie agreed and cheerfully trotted out of the room after Sara, as she would do much of the time from then on.

∽

Every so often, Sara would catch a glimpse of a girl a few years older than she was in the shadows, near the school's back entrance, or in one of its hallways. The girl was carrying heavy parcels with great difficulty. Sara knew that she was not a student. Being a curious child, she promised herself to learn more.

The other girl seemed to wonder about Sara as well, always peeking back at her with wide eyes framed by a sweet, coal-smudged face. In fact, the girl was fourteen years old, but looked only twelve because of her harsh life.

One day, she bumped into the girl in the hallway. Sara smiled at her.

When Sara smiled, people usually smiled back. But this girl seemed to get scared instead, as if she had been told that she had no business looking at—let alone smiling at—all the important young ladies.

"It's okay," Sara said kindly. "What's your name?" But the girl had already scurried away, back into the shadows.

That evening, as Sara was sitting in the parlor

telling another one of her famous stories (this one about mermaids and mermen and—oh yes—princesses), the same little girl came into the room. She was looking thin and tired, and carried a box of coal that was much too heavy.

She kneeled down to sweep up the coal ashes. She swept once, and then again. And then a third time. By then, so transported was she by Sara's story that she stopped sweeping. Instead, she slumped in a chair dreamily, letting her hearth brush hang loosely from her fingers.

Before the girl knew it, she was under the sea, with Sara and all the other important young ladies, with the mermaids and mermen. Never in her brief, hard life had sea flowers and grasses waved so gently around her, as though dancing to the music that, thanks to Sara, the little girl now heard also.

The brush fell from her hand with a loud clang. All of the girls spun around.

Lavinia looked livid. Her spiteful, stuck-up side showed through. "How dare you listen to these stories!" she demanded. "I mean, they *are* stupid stories . . . but you are only a servant girl!"

The frightened girl mumbled her apologies and, picking up her brush, ran out of the room.

"How dare *you*?" Sara stormed back at Lavinia. "Stories belong to everyone!" She was so angry that she could have slapped Lavinia. But she knew that she should behave like a true princess and not stoop to Lavinia's level.

Later, Sara found out the girl's name was Becky and that she was an orphan. Becky was the scullery maid. She worked in the kitchen below, doing messy tasks no one else would do. Often the girls could hear Miss Minchin's voice ring out from downstairs: "Becky do this" and "Becky do that." No one paid any attention, though, because it seemed to be so far removed from their rich and comfortable world.

That day, Sara vowed that she would make friends with Becky. Without thinking about it, Sara often went to the aid of people in need, and Becky was no exception.

The few times their paths crossed again, though, Becky seemed flustered. Sara knew Becky would get scolded if she were caught talking to the students, so she kept her distance.

A few weeks later, a lucky accident occurred. When Sara entered her sitting room, she found Becky in the velvet armchair by the fire. She was fast asleep, gently snoring.

Becky had come into the room to tidy it up and to add more coals to Sara's fire. Sara's room was special: cozy and colorful, and filled with pictures and books, soft blankets, and curious things from India. There was even a tiger-skin rug made from an animal her father had hunted. Becky always saved Sara's room for last as a reward for finishing her work.

Becky had never dared sit down in Sara's armchair before. But that day she thought, "I will sit down for just one minute, to rest . . ."

The warmth of the fire had enfolded her with its spell. "Just one more minute," she told herself, before quickly falling asleep.

"Oh," Sara whispered to Emily. "The poor thing! She is so tired!" Sara thought about how it was only an accident that she had such a good life, and that Becky had such a hard one. They were just two little girls, she thought, both of them more or less the same.

She didn't want to wake Becky. However, she worried that Miss Minchin might come in and find her there. Just then, a piece of burning coal fell onto the fireplace screen with a thud. Becky opened her eyes, saw Sara, and sprang up out of her chair.

"Oh, miss!" she sputtered. "I beg yer pardon!"

"Don't be sorry," Sara said. "I'm happy that you're here." Sara reached out and took Becky's hand. Although Becky was older, she seemed to need mothering as much as Lottie did.

"I didn't mean to do it, miss," Becky kept on. She was so used to being scolded that she did not even notice that Sara was being kind to her. "But the fire was so warm, an' the chair was so soft, an' I was so tired—"

"I know," Sara tried to soothe her. "And you work so hard." Becky finally could see that she was not in trouble.

"Yer really not angry, miss?" she gasped. "Yer not goin' to tell the missus?"

"Of course not," Sara said. She had another idea. "Are you done with your work?" she asked. "Can you stay a little while longer?"

Becky stared at her wide-eyed.

"Stay, miss? Me? Here?"

Sara ran to the door, checking to see if anyone was around.

"The hallway is quiet," she said. "No one knows you're here. If you are done with your work, perhaps you can visit for a while?"

Becky nodded slowly. Surely, she thought, she was still dreaming in Sara's armchair.

Sara opened a cupboard, took out a perfectly frosted chocolate cake, and cut Becky a thick slice. She smiled with pleasure as Becky ate the whole thing in what seemed like one big bite.

"Becky," Sara offered, "if you come to my room every night, I can tell you a little bit more of the mermaid story each time until the story is finished. Would you like that?"

"I would!" Becky exclaimed. "I would like that so much that I wouldn't care anymore how 'eavy the coal boxes were, or how 'ungry I was, or how mean the missus is to me. If I 'ad that to look forward to, I think I could do anything!"

And Becky did survive through the nights that followed—not only on Sara's snacks and stories, but on her warmth and kindness.

CHAPTER 3

Her Royal Highness

Two whole school years passed. Sara grew stronger and smarter and dreamed every day about returning to India to take care of her papa. Captain Crewe wrote her long and vivid letters. He also sent her books she would read late into the night, after the other girls had gone to bed.

Sara's French and her stories of India made her the perfect pupil to show off Miss Minchin's fancy boarding school. Some of the other girls began treating her as though she were royalty indeed. But others were jealous of her special attention and what they saw as fancy airs.

One day while in the parlor with her classmates, Sara received perhaps the most interesting letter of all. In it, Captain Crewe told his daughter about a new business that was sure to make them even richer than before. He had agreed to become a partner in a diamond mine with his best friend, a man he had met when he was just a boy in boarding school.

"Maybe Sara and I can have our own diamond mine someday," Ermengarde thought dreamily.

"Great," Lavinia sniffed jealously. "That's all Sara needs—*more* riches!"

"I think it sounds romantic," confessed Jessie.

Sara agreed. She didn't care about being rich. If she was excited (and she was), it was only because the idea of a diamond mine was indeed dreamy, not to mention magical. It was like something from *Arabian Nights.*

Oh, the stories the diamond mine sparked! Ermengarde, Lottie, Becky, and the other girls were treated to colorful tales of jeweled passages in the deepest parts of the earth, and of brave men digging gemstones out with picks.

"Oh, I can't bear it," Lavinia told Jessie. "Now she will *really* be stuck up."

Jessie just shrugged. She would never tell Lavinia, but she was starting to like Sara and wished her no harm.

"Did you know that Sara secretly pretends she is a *real* princess?" Lavinia asked Jessie, trying to start trouble. "Oh yes, it's true. One night I heard her telling someone—it must have been that silly dunce Ermengarde—when I was passing by her room. I think we should all start calling her 'Your Royal Highness.'"

Jessie frowned. She didn't want to call her any such thing.

Lavinia leaped up and ran over to where Sara was just finishing up her story. Much to Sara's surprise, Lavinia started to clap.

"Oh, Your Royal Highness," Lavinia said mocking her, in between claps. "Diamond mines—how exciting!"

Sara swallowed. She was rather shy about her princess fantasy (or "pretend," as she called it), and here was Lavinia making fun of it in front of the whole school.

In secret, Sara had decided that she would pretend to be a real princess. She would have real subjects (like Becky and Lottie) who needed her—the "populace," as she called them. And she would worry about more important things than just being pretty. Above all, she would try always to be generous and kind.

Sara felt like slapping Lavinia. But princesses didn't slap people, she thought. Even spiteful ones like Lavinia. She forced herself to speak calmly and, yes, regally.

"It's true," she said. "Sometimes I do pretend I am a princess. And I try to behave like one. *You* might want to try that sometimes."

"I wonder if you could still pretend you were a princess if you were a beggar girl and lived in an attic," said Lavinia with scorn.

Sara didn't know. "I would certainly try," she said.

"Hmmpf!" said Lavinia, storming out of the room in a huff.

After that, many of the other girls started fondly calling Sara "Princess." Even Miss Minchin started doing it—not fondly, but because it made visiting parents think that hers was a school for children of royalty.

Captain Crewe's letters kept coming. However, their magic had started to fade. Of course, he tried to keep the letters cheerful and full of good news. He spoke of Sara's upcoming eleventh birthday, and promised her a huge party, the likes of which the important young ladies at Miss Minchin's school had never seen.

Sara began to read between the lines of the letters: business troubles, problems with his health. Her papa seemed uneasy and spoke more often about how much he missed her—something he had always kept secret before.

On the day of her birthday, Becky came to bring Sara down to the party. Mariette quickly helped Sara finish dressing. Miss Minchin had ordered Sara to put on her finest pink silk dress, made just for the event, and to curl her hair. Sara hadn't wanted to make such a fuss, but Miss Minchin had insisted. Because Captain Crewe would be paying her back for the party many times over, she would see to it that no expense was spared.

Becky walked Sara to the parlor-turned-party

room. Instead of leaving then, however, as she knew she ought to, Becky could not help but stay and look at the colorful party decorations, the lovely cakes, and the piles of presents.

Miss Minchin spotted Becky. "Servant girl!" she snapped. "Leave us this instant!"

"Oh please, Miss Minchin," Sara begged, "can't Becky stay, as a special favor to me on my birthday? After all, Becky is a little girl, too."

Miss Minchin was visibly upset. She had always thought of Becky more as a machine than as a little girl. But it would not do for Sara to tell her rich father that she had been refused. Once again, Sara had made her feel oddly uncomfortable, and she didn't know quite why.

"Fine," Miss Minchin said, frowning. She waved to Becky. "Go stand over there, but not too near the young ladies."

Becky bounded happily to the corner where Miss Minchin had pointed.

Becky wasn't the only one hungrily eyeing the cakes. But Miss Minchin allowed no one to take a single bite, or open a single present, until they all sang "Happy Birthday."

"On the count of three," Miss Minchin instructed, "we will begin." She hit her tuning fork to give the key.

"Happy birth—" they all began.

All of a sudden, they were interrupted when Miss Amelia burst clumsily into the room.

"Amelia!" Miss Minchin yelled. Now they would have to start again.

"I'm sorry," Miss Amelia said, out of breath. "But it is an urgent matter. At least Mr. Barrow says so. He needs to talk to you right away."

"Who?" Miss Minchin asked impatiently.

"Mr. Barrow—waiting to speak to you in your office," Miss Amelia sputtered. "He says he is Captain Crewe's business manager."

Miss Minchin's ears perked up.

"Well it's about time,"she thought. "I have spent hundreds of pounds on that little princess since she's been here, and at least a hundred on this silly party alone, and it has been months now since I have been paid back a penny."

She fish-smiled so widely that she looked like a giant flounder. She told the young ladies she would be right back. Feeling very generous at the thought of receiving such a large check, she even told the students that they could start eating. They would finish singing to Sara when she returned.

CHAPTER 4

The Change

Mr. Barrow," Miss Minchin exclaimed as she swept graciously into her office. "I am *so delighted* to see you again!"

But when Mr. Barrow stood up to greet her, he did not look happy.

"Miss Minchin," he told her, looking grave, "perhaps you should sit down."

Miss Minchin went stiff. "Is something wrong?" she asked.

"That," Mr. Barrow said, sitting down, "is putting it rather mildly."

Mr. Barrow then revealed what he had come to tell her: how the diamond mines had failed, and about the late Captain Crewe.

"Excuse me," Miss Minchin gasped. "The *late* Captain Crewe?"

"He's dead, ma'am," Mr. Barrow confirmed. "He died of jungle fever and bad business. But that's not the half of it."

"There's more?" Miss Minchin asked.

"Captain Crewe died without a cent, quite out of his mind, raving about his little girl."

Miss Minchin could hardly breathe—not from pity, mind you, but out of anger. She felt that, somehow, she had been cheated out of what was rightfully hers. Cheated by the late Captain Crewe, by Barrow and Skipworth, even by Sara.

She spoke slowly. "Are you telling me . . . that he left the child *nothing*? That he left *me* nothing? That Sara is in there right now, having a grand party at my expense, for which I shall never see *one penny*?"

"Yes, I'm afraid the child is a beggar." Mr. Barrow did not mince words. "But before you think of turning her out into the street, think about how that would look for your school. And by the way," he added dryly, "Barrow and Skipworth is not responsible for her—you are."

Miss Minchin could not believe her ears. But her mind was indeed working at top speed. She was nothing if not a shrewd businesswoman and knew just what Mr. Barrow meant. After a long silence, she spoke.

"Yes—better to keep her," she agreed, "and to make use of her." Her eyes narrowed shrewdly. "I can assure you, sir, that I will make good use of her!"

Their conversation was cut short by the sound of singing. It was the students, Miss Minchin thought foggily. They had started without her. She ran back down the hall.

"Stop your singing this minute!" she

screamed with fury. She threw open the door and rushed into the room. "Everybody quiet!"

The startled girls stopped in midchorus.

"Sara Crewe!" Miss Minchin ordered. "Come here this instant!"

The crowd parted, and Sara walked quietly to the front of the room.

"Yes, Miss Minchin," she replied.

"Do you have a black frock in your grand princess wardrobe?" Miss Minchin asked in a mocking tone.

"Why, I'm sure that Sara has a frock in every color," Lavinia said under her breath.

"A black frock?" Miss Amelia repeated. "Sister, what *are* you talking about?"

"I have an old black velvet dress," Sara said timidly, "but I have outgrown it. It is too short."

"That is too bad," Miss Minchin said. "Go take off that ridiculous pink thing and put the black one on. You are done with finery!"

In shock, the other girls became speechless.

"Sister, what has happened?" Miss Amelia cried. Miss Minchin did not mince words.

"Captain Crewe is dead," she said. "He died penniless, leaving this spoiled little princess on my hands."

The girls let out a gasp. Miss Amelia fell heavily into the nearest chair. Becky, still standing at the party's edges, started to cry. But Sara was another story: she actually made no fuss at all. Although her eyes got quite big and she turned pale, she stood very still and looked at Miss Minchin without saying a word, before turning and walking silently out of the room.

Looking around at what was left of the lavish party, Miss Minchin was enraged.

"Girls!" she ordered. "Put down your cake and go back to your rooms *right now*!"

She turned to face Becky, whose face was streaming with tears.

"And you," she said, "stop your wailing and clean up this mess. This party is over!"

Upstairs, a trembling Mariette was helping Sara to change into the old black dress Miss Minchin had ordered her to put on. Mariette had also grown very fond of Sara, and feared it would be the last thing she was allowed to do for the girl. Sara hardly seemed to notice Mariette.

"My papa is dead," she kept saying quietly to herself alone. "My papa is dead."

Emily, too, had been draped in a piece of black cloth. Mariette had thought it fitting.

"Oh, Emily!" Sara cried. "Do you hear? Papa is dead! He died in India, thousands of miles away!"

Emily seemed to break the rules for a second and to come to life, only to stare sadly at Sara from her nearby chair. But then the second passed, and once again Emily seemed like nothing more than a piece of porcelain, with cloth-and-sawdust legs.

"My papa is dead!" Sara screamed, shaking her doll. But Emily just flopped around limply in Sara's hands.

A heartbroken rage seized Sara like never before. She burst into tears and threw Emily to the ground, half hoping she would break.

"My papa is dead, and you are nothing but a doll!" she cried. "A doll—a doll—a doll!"

Emily lay on the floor, with her legs twisted strangely over her head and a newly flattened tip at the end of her nose. Still she seemed calm, even dignified.

Regret overtook Sara, and she rushed over to pick Emily up. The doll seemed to come to life again in part, looking up at Sara with glassy-eyed sympathy.

"I'm sorry," Sara said, with a weary sigh. "I'm sure you are doing your sawdust best."

Then one of the girls knocked on Sara's door

with a message. Miss Minchin had called Sara back downstairs.

Sara was still holding on to Emily when she entered Miss Minchin's office.

"What do you mean bringing your doll in here?" Miss Minchin demanded. "Put her down."

"No," Sara answered. "She is all that I have. My papa gave her to me as a companion."

Miss Minchin wanted to grab the doll from Sara, but she couldn't. Sara had always made her feel secretly ill at ease, and with Sara's steady gaze, she was doing so even now. Truth be told, Miss Minchin was a little afraid of Sara then, because she knew in her heart what an unkind thing she was about to do.

"You will have no time for dolls anymore," she said coldly. "Your life as you have known it is over. You are all alone in the world."

For a moment, Sara's thin, pale little face

twitched, but still she said nothing. She did not cry or seem at all frightened. Her bravery was too much for Miss Minchin to bear.

"What are you staring at?" she asked sharply. "Why do you not speak? Don't you understand what I am telling you? You, with all of your grand airs, are now a beggar. You will work here to earn your keep and to pay me back for everything you owe me."

"I understand," Sara replied in a low tone. "Now, may I please be excused?"

She turned slowly to leave the room.

"Stop!" Miss Minchin said. "Aren't you going to thank me?"

Sara paused, surprised, and looked at Miss Minchin oddly. "What for?" she asked.

"Well, for my kindness to you, of course," Miss Minchin replied. "For allowing you to stay here. For giving you a home."

A fierce feeling of pride suddenly surged up in

Sara. "You are not kind," she said, "and this will never be my home!" Clutching Emily tightly, she turned and ran out of Miss Minchin's office and back up to her room.

When she reached her door, however, she found Miss Amelia blocking it.

"I'm sorry, but this is not your room anymore." Miss Amelia blushed from shame at having to carry out her sister's orders. "You are to sleep in the attic, in the room next to Becky's." Sara could see this was the beginning of the change Miss Minchin had foretold.

Sara knew where the attic was. Becky had spoken to her about it many times. And so she turned and walked up the extra two flights of stairs. As she did so, she felt as though she were leaving behind everything she had ever known or been. When she got to the top of the stairs, she felt like a completely different creature.

Her new room had a slanted ceiling. The walls

were covered in peeling paint. There was a hard bed covered with a thin and faded quilt, a tiny rusty fireplace, and just a few other pieces of faded and worn-out furniture. Under the window, with its broken glass, there stood a red footstool with a broken leg. Sara went over to it and sat down. She put her face down, hugged herself, and just rocked. Still, she did not cry.

A low tap came at the door, followed by a face peeping timidly around the corner. It was Becky's face, which, in addition to being smudgy, was now also quite red from crying.

"Oh miss," she said. "Might I come in? Is there anything I can do for you? Please, will you still let me wait on you?"

Sara looked up. She had intended to smile, but when she saw the love and sadness in Becky's face, something broke inside of her. Finally, the tears came.

"Oh, Becky," she sobbed. "Thank you, but no,

there is nothing anyone can do. You will never wait on me again, you see? I was right—both of us are only two little girls, just alike. I'm not a princess anymore."

Becky ran over and kneeled beside Sara to hug her. "Yes, miss, you are," she cried. "Whatever happens, you'll always be a princess. Nothin' could make you any different!"

CHAPTER 5

Proud Soldiers Don't Complain

Sara's first night in the attic was the scariest of her life.

The room itself was frightful enough, with its bare wood floor, its hard bed, and the wind howling overhead. But the toenail scratchings and shrill little squeaks coming from the walls were even scarier. She knew these were the rats.

The most terrifying thing of all, however, was the idea that her papa could really be dead: that she would never see him again, and that she was all alone in the world. No matter how many times she repeated it to herself, she still could not believe it.

Miss Minchin, however, would be very helpful in convincing her.

The next morning, Sara walked past the open door to what used to be her room. She caught a glimpse inside and saw that everything had been removed or changed. As if by some evil magician, any trace of the girl she used to be, and the life she used to lead when her papa was alive, had been erased—just like that. Miss Minchin must have taken all her finery to be sold to pay for her party, thought Sara.

She didn't like thinking unkind thoughts about magic, or about grown-ups for that matter. Magic and pretend had always been her favorite things, her biggest source of strength, but now it seemed that no amount of magic or make-believe could help her.

"Your new life begins today," Miss Minchin

informed her when she went downstairs. "You will work for me, in exchange for my kindness of not turning you out onto the street. You will begin by overseeing the younger girls, teaching them French and other subjects."

That, Sara thought, would not be so bad. She loved spending time with the younger girls and teaching them things, and their warm affection for her also gave Sara joy. Little did she know, however, that it was only the beginning of her toil.

Miss Minchin would also send Sara on errands, at any time of day or night, and in the worst weather. She would have Sara deliver grown-up messages to people in town and pay her bills. An errand boy would never have been so clever or reliable. Although Sara was a slight little girl, the cook often sent her out to buy groceries. Sara carried them back through the streets with a heavy basket on her arm. Miss Minchin ordered Sara to do all of the hard, unpleasant tasks the other servants would not do.

As for the other servants, the cook and the housemaids, although they, too, were servants, it was easy to boss around the youngest and newest among them. Sara used to put on what they considered fancy airs, and Miss Minchin seemed to dislike her as well, so they thought that such treatment was fitting.

Sara tried to remain strong and not to complain. She hoped that they all would see that she was a hard worker and would soften and be kinder toward her over time.

But she was wrong. The harder she tried to please them and do as she was told, the meaner and more demanding everyone became.

She grew sadder and lonelier as each day passed. The worst thing was going outside and seeing other people. When she had been Princess Sara, just the sight of her bright and eager face had caused people to smile, especially when she was back in India.

But no one looked at her anymore. In fact, if they saw her by chance, they seemed to want to look away as quickly as possible. She must really have been a sight.

Sometimes, when it was dark, she would stop in front of windows that were all lit up, and peer into the warm rooms filled with happy families. One family that seemed particularly happy lived in the same square as the school, two houses away. Sara called them the Large Family, not because the members of it were particularly large, but because there were so many of them—eight children in all. All eight of them, and their parents, too, seemed happy and fond of each other and of the world. They were always telling jokes, giving each other little gifts, and going on outings together.

The house right next door to the school had

stood empty for a while. But soon those windows would be lit up as well. One day, when returning from her errands, she saw to her great delight a van parked in front of the house next door. She had an idea that, if she could see some of the furniture, she could guess something about the new neighbors.

The furniture that was being delivered to this house looked familiar to Sara. It was teakwood, and other pieces covered with rich Oriental embroidery. Why, she had seen things just like these in India! She wondered if the single man, her new next-door neighbor, was from India as well. When she looked inside, she saw not a large happy family, but one lonely man. He was the Little Family, Sara thought to herself, for no number was littler than one.

When Mr. Large stopped by to say hello to the new neighbor, she wondered if the Large Family and the Lonely-Family-of-One were friends. She hoped so, for her new neighbor's sake. But most of all she wondered why, when she caught a glimpse of him through a lighted window, Mr. Little seemed to appear as she felt—sickly and sad. Perhaps he was missing someone, too, as her father had so missed his "Little Missus" before he died?

One of the things that Sara loved, her schoolwork, became harder and harder.

"Servants don't need schooling," Miss Minchin said. What she meant is that servants don't have the right to be given lessons. Even so, Sara was expected, after long and busy days spent doing everybody's bidding, to go into the deserted and darkened schoolroom to study alone at night. Often she would fall asleep over her books and be awakened the next morning with a slap and a scolding. If she didn't keep up, she may not have been kept on as a teacher of the older classes. That was the future Sara had to look forward to at Miss Minchin's school.

The biggest change, however, came in the way the other girls treated her. Whereas once they had been drawn to her in admiration, now they were awkward and uncertain, especially as her one black dress grew shorter and shabbier, her shoes developed holes, and her face grew paler and thinner. After a time, she was told to eat in the kitchen with the other servants.

Although saddened by their treatment of her, Sara was far too proud to try to win the girls back. Her heart grew even stiffer and sorer than her body. She never told anyone about how she felt inside, thinking, "Soldiers don't complain."

Some days, however, it seemed that her heart would break with loneliness. Even her old friend Ermengarde seemed to have let her down. Weeks went by, after the change, before she saw Ermengarde at all. One day, however, while her arms were full of garments to be mended, she bumped into her former best friend in the hall.

Ermengarde just stood and stared, her pouty mouth wide open. She stared because she never imagined that Sara could look so odd and poor, like a servant girl. She felt like crying, but was so upset and nervous that instead she broke into a short fit of laughter and stupidly asked, "Oh Sara, is that you?"

"Yes," Sara said, shortly, her face flushing.

"Oh," Ermengarde started, overcome with shyness. "How—are you?"

Sara had never lost patience with poor, dull Ermengarde before, but all at once it seemed that Ermengarde was no better than the other girls who had left her all alone.

Sara lost her self-control. "How do you think I am?" she snapped. "You really *are* stupid, aren't you!" Her heart broke at her own meanness, and at the horrible look of shame and sadness that crossed over Ermengarde's face. With that, Sara turned and walked away.

After that meeting, Sara tried to stay away from the other girls altogether. Miss Minchin made that easy enough. Sometimes Sara would see Ermengarde sitting alone in a window seat, huddled up in a corner crying, and she felt like rushing over and saying she was sorry. But she was too proud, and so she held herself back.

At least, she thought, she still had Becky. Becky was one of the few comforts in her hard new life. They had no time or right, of course, to speak to each other during the day. But before dawn, Becky sometimes slipped into Sara's room to say hello, and to help her in any way that she could. And at night, Becky would come to visit again, always knocking first, humbly, at Sara's door.

"Will you still let me be yer handmaid, miss?" Becky kept asking.

But Sara always firmly told her no. "We are the same," she said again. "We are just two little servant girls, living in the attic."

Just then, an interesting thing happened. Sara's imagination, which had for weeks been shocked into some kind of deep sleep, seemed briefly to flicker awake. Becky noticed it, too.

"What is it, miss?" Becky whispered.

"I was wrong," Sara said, her eyes shining. "We are more than mere servants. We are two poor old prisoners. It is the French Revolution, and we have been captured and thrown into the Bastille prison in Paris!" Sara exclaimed. "Miss Minchin is our jailor, and you are the prisoner in the next cell!"

"Oh I am, miss," Becky agreed, secretly thrilled. She was happy not so much at the thought of being a prisoner, but at the thought that Sara, and her stories, had returned to life.

CHAPTER 6

The Visitors

One night, several lonely weeks later, a weary Sara reached the top of the attic stairs. She was surprised to see a flicker of candlelight coming from under her door.

She opened the door to find Ermengarde, dressed in her nightgown and wrapped in a red shawl, sitting on the crooked footstool. When Ermengarde looked up, Sara could see that her eyes and nose were pink from crying.

"Ermengarde!" cried Sara. "You shouldn't be here. You will get into trouble."

"I know," Ermengarde said, "but I don't care." She squeezed her eyes shut and two big fat tears rolled out, down her pink cheeks. "Oh Sara, please tell me," she begged. "Why don't you like me anymore?"

A lump rose up in Sara's throat.

"But I *do* like you," she answered. "I thought it was *you* that didn't like *me* anymore!"

The two girls rushed into each other's arms. For the first time ever, Ermengarde let go first. Only then did Sara realize how lonely she had been without her best friend.

"I couldn't stand it anymore," Ermengarde said. "I had to come up here and beg you to be friends again."

"You are nicer than I am," Sara said. "I missed you, too, but I was too proud to say anything." She frowned. "You see? Now that my luck has run out, I've discovered that I am not so nice after all."

Ermengarde glanced around the attic room

with both fear and curiosity. "How can you bear living up here?" she asked.

Sara looked around as well. She found that she was actually getting used to it.

"I just try to pretend that I am someplace else," she said. "For a while I couldn't pretend at all, or tell stories—not even to myself." She nodded in her serious way. "But it's all coming back to me now, slowly but surely."

Sara told Ermengarde about how she and Becky and Emily were prisoners in the Bastille prison. Ermengarde was instantly drawn in. She had sorely missed Sara's storytelling.

"Will you tell me more about the Bastille?" she asked. "May I sneak up here at night sometimes, when it is safe, and visit you?"

Sara told her she could, if she was careful.

Suddenly, however, both girls saw the doorknob to the attic room turning. Who could it be? they wondered in suspense. Miss Minchin? Miss

Amelia? Or one of the older girls, like Lavinia, who would surely tell on them? When the door opened, however, it was none other than little Lottie. Today, it seemed, was to be chock-full of visitors.

Although flustered, Sara was not entirely surprised to see her little "adopted" daughter. Lottie, who was still only seven, was quite confused about the sudden change in her make-believe mother. She had tried to get Sara to tell her where she had been taken and why.

Sara had refused to tell her, but Lottie was one stubborn little girl. She had listened in on the older girls' gossip about Sara. This evening, she started on her voyage of discovery. She climbed stairs she never knew existed—so many stairs that she thought her little legs would fall off—until she reached the attic and saw the light under Sara's door.

At first, she was overjoyed to have found Sara.

But when she saw the bare and ugly room, her face fell. "Mama Sara!" she cried in horror. She seemed as if she might start wailing and flailing again—something she had not done in a long time. "Surely you don't live here?"

"Please, Lottie," Sara begged. "Don't make too much noise, or I will be yelled at for sure, and I have been yelled at all day." She forced a smile. "Besides," she offered, "it isn't such a bad room."

"It isn't?" Lottie asked, glancing around once more, looking uncertain. "Why not?"

"Quite right," Ermengarde added, looking as confused as Lottie. She had forgotten all about the storybook romance of the Bastille prison.

"Well," Sara began, "for starters, I am lucky to live in an attic that has windows. Not all attics do, you know. And you can see all sorts of things out these windows that you can't see from downstairs."

"What sorts of things?" Lottie asked.

"Why, enchanting roofs and railings covered in soot," Sara began, "and chimneys with smoke curling up out of them in wonderful designs. And friendly sparrows, chirping for crumbs. And the rain's big fat drops falling from the sky and going pitter-patter upon the slate roof like gumdrops. And such splendid sunsets! Dazzling bright red and gold ones, or little fleecy, floating clouds hurrying across the blue sky, riding the waves of the wind. And other attic windows, like that one just across the way." Sara pointed. Lottie and Ermengarde looked out at the building next door. "Where other heads might peek out at any minute."

Sara paused, also staring out at the attic window across the way. It was so close, separated only by a stretch of roof. Someone with good balance might easily walk across it. But as hard as she had wished, nobody had ever walked across to keep her company.

"My room is so little and high above everything," she continued, trying to get back on a cheery note, "that it is like a wonderful nest in a tree. And when I lie in bed and look out the windows, I feel as if I could surely touch the clouds and the stars."

Ermengarde had no doubt that Sara could.

"What else?" Lottie whispered.

"Well," Sara said, "just look at that rusty fireplace. If it were polished and there was a fire in it, just think how lovely it would be." She sighed and closed her eyes. "Just imagine a soft, thick, blue Indian rug on the floor, and a cozy couch in that corner with cushions to curl up on. Picture a bookshelf just over the couch, full of wonderful storybooks, and a fur rug before the fire, and lamps, and drawings on the wall, and warm delicious food spread out like a picnic . . .

"And on the bed," Sara finished (for she was getting quite tired), "there would be a soft and warm silk coverlet. I would lie down on it and have such wonderful dreams!"

Their flight of fancy was interrupted by a loud scratching coming from the walls.

"What's that?" both Ermengarde and Lottie exclaimed at once.

Sara smiled. "Oh that," she said. "That's just Melchisedec, my pet rat."

"Your *imaginary* pet rat?" Ermengarde asked nervously, clutching her red shawl more tightly around her.

"No," Sara said. She then explained how, during the past weeks, when she was sure she had no friends left in the world, she had made friends with a rat. She had named him Melchisedec. He was, she had realized, quite shy and sweet, and as afraid of her as she had been of him. All it had taken was a few spare crumbs saved from the kitchen to win him over.

"It is just like a story," Lottie whispered.

"Why of course it is," Sara replied. "Everything is a story!"

As fascinated as they were by Melchisedec the rat, no one realized that just a few minutes earlier, another head had indeed appeared in the attic window across the way, at long last. It was the white-turbaned, dark-faced head of a native Indian manservant—a *lascar*, Sara would have called him, had she seen him.

Since both attic windows were open, the *lascar* could hear everything that was being said. But lest he forget even one tiny detail, he was bent over a notepad, scribbling carefully.

Although heartened by their visit with Sara, Ermengarde and Lottie could not risk staying longer. Hugging their friend good-bye, they slipped back down the stairs.

"Everything is a story," Sara repeated to herself. However, looking around the attic once more, the magic of her stories, told for the other girls' sakes, had for the most part died away. Everything became hard and bare again. Emily was only a doll again; not even Melchisedec could comfort her. "Oh, it's a lonely place," she sighed. "It's the loneliest place in the world!"

The *lascar*, still listening from across the way, didn't need to write down this saying. He would never forget how sad and lonely this little girl was. In fact, she reminded him of his employer, the Indian gentleman downstairs, who was searching for a little girl about Sarah's age. They had many things in common, he thought. Perhaps, he thought next, something could be done to help both of them.

Before going to bed, Sara gently knocked three times on the wall in a code she had created with Becky. It meant, "Prisoner, are you there?"

After a minute, three knocks could be heard from the other side. They meant, "Yes, I am here, and all is well." This was never quite true, but the girls always said it anyway.

Sara knocked just one more time, a fourth. This meant, "Then, fellow-sufferer, we will sleep in peace. Good night."

The next morning, Sara was looking out the window, hoping to catch a glimpse of the sunrise, when there came a funny squeaking sound from across the way. It sounded like a giant Melchisedec, somewhere up on the roof. But when Sara looked out, she saw not a Melchisedec but a monkey, popping up in the open window like a jack-in-the-box.

Behind the monkey, there suddenly appeared another surprise: the delightful, smiling face of a *lascar* wrapped in a white turban. "A monkey and a *lascar* . . . ," Sara wondered. "Could I be dreaming? Have I died and gone back to the heaven that was India?"

Before she could answer her own questions, both she and the *lascar* watched as the playful monkey scurried across the rooftop and opened Sara's window. Jumping in, the monkey started to scamper crazily all over her attic room.

But Sara wasn't scared. She had been around many monkeys in India, and this lively little baby only made her laugh. She also knew that the monkey must return to his master. She turned in the *lascar*'s direction, glad that she still remembered some of the Hindu dialect she had learned

while in India with her father. "Will he let me catch him?" she asked him in Hindi.

She thought she had never seen more surprise and delight than she did at that moment, in the *lascar*'s face.

"Probably not," the *lascar* replied, in beautifully accented English. He introduced himself to her, making a polite and elegant bow. "My name is Ram Dass," he said. "The monkey is sweet," he added, "but as unruly as a small child, and hard to catch. But may I come across the roof and stand at the edge of your window and call to him? He will probably leap straight into my arms."

Sara looked over her shoulder at the little monkey, who was darting across the room as though frightened. "Please do," she said, afraid that the monkey would hurt himself.

Ram Dass was right. As soon as the monkey caught sight of his master's handsome, white-turbaned head, he hopped first onto Sara's shoulder and then back out through the window. Before he vanished, he turned to give Sara a little thank-you scream.

"Glad to be of service," Sara replied with a laugh.

But Ram Dass was not amused. Through the window, his quick eyes had taken in at one glance all of the bare drabness of Sara's room: it was no laughing matter that a little girl should be allowed to live this way. However, he did not reveal his true feelings. When he spoke to her, he might as well have been speaking to the daughter of an Indian *rajah*.

He apologized for any trouble the monkey may have caused her. "My employer is quite ill," he explained, "and this little mischief maker gives him much pleasure." At that, he raised his hand in a greeting of peace and smiled. Then he recrossed the slate roof to his own window as sure-footedly as the monkey himself.

CHAPTER 7

The Little Girl Who Was Not a Beggar

After he had gone, Sara stood in the middle of her room and let all sorts of memories wash over her. The *lascar* had brought them back for her—especially when he had spoken to her so nicely, as though she were still a little princess and had a divine right to her place in the world.

While some of her make-believe stories had come back to her in these recent hard days—and indeed had saved her life, she thought—there had been one "pretend" that she still could not bring back to life. And that was the princess pretend. Not even an expert pretender, she had thought, could make that one real in her present situation.

But somehow, seeing the *lascar* and the monkey made her strong once again. "Even if I am a pretend princess in rags and tatters," she thought, "I can still be a true princess—inside."

And from then on, that's what she did. When someone treated her rudely, Sara would simply fix her eyes upon them and smile.

"You don't know that you are saying and doing these things to a princess," she would think to herself. "If I chose to, I could send you off to jail with a wave of my hand. I spare you only because I am a princess, and because you are a poor, stupid, mean old thing who doesn't know any better!"

One time, when Sara was thinking these things, Miss Minchin almost seemed to read her mind. For some reason (that Miss Minchin herself was unaware of), she reached out and boxed Sara's ears in full view of the other girls.

"Sister!" Miss Amelia was in shock. It seemed to her that Sara had just been standing there, doing nothing. And while her sister often boxed Sara's ears (and Becky's, too), never had she done so in the schoolroom. "Why did you do that? Did Sara say something smart-mouthed?"

"Well, no," Miss Minchin admitted. "But she was *thinking* something—I'm sure of it!" Her eyes turned into slits as she stared at Sara.

"You were thinking something rude—confess it!"

"I was," Sara said steadily.

"How dare you think?" Miss Minchin screeched.

This was such a silly remark that a few of the girls started to giggle.

Miss Minchin turned red. "I mean," she corrected herself, "*what* were you thinking?"

Sara thought perhaps it would be dangerous to reply to Miss Minchin, but felt it her duty to give an honest answer.

"I was wondering how you would feel," she began in a slow, serious way, "if you found out that I really *was* a princess. I wondered if you would feel scared, or regret the fact that you had kept a true princess up in your attic, and had been treating her ill the whole time."

All the other girls were listening closely. Not a sound could be heard as they waited with keen interest for Miss Minchin's answer.

"Go to your room this instant!" Miss Minchin cried, out of breath. She felt as though she might faint. How could she feel so defeated by such an uppity little girl? She became enraged and could no longer control it. She turned to the students. "And you, young ladies, attend to your lessons!"

"Did you see her proud little face?" Jessie said to Lavinia, who seemed as oddly stirred by Sara's comment as Miss Minchin was. "I wouldn't be at all surprised if she *did* turn out to be someone important! I almost hope she does!"

One evening, a very strange thing happened. The Large children were going to a party. They were getting into their carriage when Sara passed by. Veronica Eustacia Large and Rosalind Gladys Large (Sara had made up these names), in lovely dresses with sashes, had just climbed into the carriage, with little Guy Clarence Large, aged five, behind them.

He was such a cute little boy, with rosy chubby cheeks and blue eyes, that Sara forgot about her basket and her shabby, odd appearance. Instead of hurrying past, as she had lately been doing in public, she paused to look at Guy Clarence for a moment.

Guy Clarence looked right back. It was Christmastime, and his parents had told him that there were poor children in the world who had no lovely Christmas presents or warm and delicious Christmas dinners. This story had made Guy Clarence so sad that he had vowed to find one such poor child, and give her the coins he had been keeping in his pocket. Guy Clarence didn't know much about money. He thought that his small treasure might make someone rich and, generous little soul that he was, he was glad to do it. And Sara seemed like the perfect choice.

"Here, my poor little girl," Guy Clarence said, reaching into his pocket for the coins. "Here are my life savings. I will give them to you."

Sara blinked, and all at once realized that she looked like the poor beggar children she had seen in her better days. Her face turned red and then pale.

"Oh no!" she replied. "I mean, thank you, but no. I simply couldn't accept it."

Her voice was so unlike an ordinary poor beggar child's that Veronica Eustacia (whose real name was Janet) and Rosalind Gladys (who was really Nora) leaned forward to listen.

"Please listen, poor little beggar girl," Guy Clarence pleaded. His lower lip shook and, somewhat Lottie-like, he looked as if he might start to cry. "You can buy food with it. Aren't you hungry?"

Little did he know that what she really hungered for, even more than food, was the warm and merry life that the Large children enjoyed. But Sara was hungry. And Guy Clarence was so well meaning and kind that she knew it would be impolite to refuse him. So she reached out, took the coins, and put them into her pocket along with her pride.

"Thank you, Guy Clarence," she said, giving him a little hug. "You are a kind, darling little boy!" And with that, she rushed away, blinking back her tears as she went.

"Why did she call me Guy Clarence?" the boy asked. (His real name was Donald.)

"And why did she speak so nicely?" Janet asked. "A beggar girl would have said, 'Thank yer kindly, sir,' grabbed the coins, and perhaps bobbed a little curtsy."

"I think she is a servant at that school in the square," Nora said, "but she is surely not a beggar, however shabby she looks."

From then on, the Large Family became just as interested in Sara as she was in them. Not knowing her real name, either, they dubbed her "The Little Girl Who Is Not a Beggar."

CHAPTER 8

The Other Side of the Wall

In the kitchen, it was a mystery how the servants knew and gossiped about everything. There, Sara learned more about the Indian gentleman who had moved in next door. He had come from India, but he was really an Englishman who had been living in India only while he worked on a new business. He had become quite ill with brain fever, and had still not fully gotten better. For a time, it had seemed that his entire fortune was lost, and he had almost died from shame, along with his sickness.

His fortune had changed, though, and all that he owned had been given back to him. Still, knowing that he had let down his old school chum and the little girl was too much to bear.

Sara felt butterflies in her stomach.

The Indian gentleman's story was so much like her own papa's that, if she hadn't seen him for herself, she might have thought they were one and the same person. She was glad (at least for the Englishman's sake) that his story had turned out happier. From then on, the Indian gentleman held a special place in her heart.

When she was sent out at night to fetch things, instead of grumbling, she was now eager. It gave her a better chance of spotting her new secret friend through his lighted window, as he gazed sadly into the fire. At night, she would lie awake wondering about him. She wished that he had a little daughter, a "Little Missus" all his own, who could pamper him the way she had pampered her papa. Oh, her dear papa! It seemed like ages since she had sat at his knee talking of important things. It was worlds away.

Meanwhile, right next door, on the other side of the wall, the Indian gentleman was lost in his own thoughts.

Mr. Carrisford (for that was his real name) was thinking that he ought to feel happier. After all, he was a very lucky man. After a period of forgetfulness caused by the brain fever, when he thought he had lost everything, his fortune had been returned, and his brain was just about back to normal as well. He had made many friends, including Mr. Carmichael next door (the head of the Large Family in real life). And Mr. Carmichael's little girls, especially Janet and Nora, were such a joy to him. They visited often and brought him sweets and told him funny stories about their day.

One time, they told him a quite unusual story,

although it was hardly funny. They told him about their encounter with The Little Girl Who Is Not a Beggar. Ram Dass happened to hear what the girls were saying, and he came over to add to their story.

"Why, that must be the same little girl who lives in the attic next door!" He then described Sara's bare attic room with its worn-out floor-boards and broken plaster, its rusty and empty fireplace grate, and its hard, narrow bed.

"I wonder how many poor little servant girls there are out there," Carrisford asked, "sleeping on such hard, awful beds while we lie peacefully on our feather pillows?" The thought seemed to sink him into an even deeper mire of sadness.

"My dear friend," begged Mr. Carmichael, who had arrived to pick up his daughters. "You must try not to think about such things. You are still in a weakened state—please try to rest and not upset yourself so."

But Mr. Carrisford could not stop thinking of Sara and her pitiful attic room.

"Do you suppose," he said slowly after a pause, "that the other child—" ("the child I never stop thinking of and searching for," he thought) "—could be out there somewhere, in a similar place, and in such misery?"

Mr. Carmichael didn't know what to say. He knew, of course, what his friend was talking about. But there were no easy answers.

Mr. Carrisford had told him the whole story about Captain Crewe and his daughter. Mr. Carrisford had gone to India to embark on an exciting new diamond mine business. He had invited his old school chum, Captain Ralph Crewe, to be his partner.

Things had been going smoothly until both men had fallen ill with jungle fever, which affects the mind. The fever had hit Carrisford particularly hard. He went so crazy that he was sure the business had failed. Half mad, and scared by the thought of losing both men's money, he could not face his best friend. He had run away and ended up in a hospital somewhere, where he did not wake up for weeks. Or at least, so he was told.

Of course, when he did wake up, his best friend was already dead and buried.

"He died thinking that I had made him a pauper and then run away!" he told Carmichael, his face full of pain.

It was already a sad story, but that wasn't the worst part. Carrisford's friend Crewe also had a little girl. Crewe had often talked about his daughter, and Carrisford knew that the child was away in a boarding school somewhere, waiting for her father to call her back to India. But that was all he knew. He did not know what city the boarding school was in, or even what country. It could have been Paris, London, or anywhere else in Europe.

Worst of all, he did not know even the little girl's name. Her father had only spoken of her as his "Little Missus." She was out there somewhere, no doubt suffering. And he could do nothing about it.

"Come now," said Carmichael, trying to comfort his friend. "It is a shame, yes, that the little girl in Paris turned out to be the wrong little girl. But we will never stop looking for her. We shall search high and low, and we will find her yet. In fact, in a few days' time, I am going to follow up on the clue you were given and go to Russia to look for her in Moscow."

"Thank you," poor Carrisford cried out, reaching for his friend's hand. "If I were a healthy man, I would go myself, but . . . I must find the Little Missus, I simply must!"

"Until then," Ram Dass advised, "perhaps we can help the Little Missus right next door? What do you think, sir?"

Carrisford's eyes lit up and he sat taller in his chair. "What do you suggest?" he asked.

Ram Dass smiled, pulled out a small notepad, and drew his chair closer. "Well, for starters, we might try a little redecorating."

The next afternoon, while Sara was out working, Melchisedec was also busy. His job was to scour Sara's room for any spare crumbs that she might have dropped. Melchisedec had learned that, no matter how little his roommate had to eat, she always left a tiny bit for him.

Sara's room may not have been great for a little girl, but it was perfectly pleasant for a rat. For starters, it was usually quiet.

But on this day, there was a ruckus. It began with the sound of something moving on the roof, coming toward the window. Then there was the sound of the window creaking open.

Melchisedec ran behind the wall and peeked out from his tiny hole. He could see two faces peering into the window, both filled with caution and interest. It was Ram Dass and another young man: Carrisford's secretary. But of course, Melchisedec didn't know this. He stood perfectly still and shook, well—like a mouse.

When slipping through the window after Ram Dass, the secretary caught a glimpse of Melchisedec's shaking tail.

"Is that a rat?" he asked Ram Dass in a frightened whisper.

"Yes," Ram Dass replied, "but the child is not afraid. She is the little friend of all things."

"You seem to know much about her," observed the secretary.

"I do know her," Ram Dass agreed. "I often watch her from my own window, to make sure that she is safe. I observe her in her sadness and her poor joys, her cold, and her hunger. I know when her friends sneak up to visit her, and I know when they leave and she cries herself to sleep. Finally, because I can sometimes hear her through the open window, I know the things that she pretends in order to survive."

"And her pretend world—that is why we're here?" The secretary tried hard to understand.

"Exactly," Ram Dass smiled.

Ram Dass took out his notepad again. He had already written several pages of notes on Sara since that day when he overheard Sara telling Ermengarde and Lottie everything that the attic could be, if they only pretended.

"Thick, soft, blue Indian rug," he had written, and "Cozy couch." "Tiger-skin rug in front of fire," he had put down below that, and then, "Lamps; pictures on the wall."

"Why, this bed is awful!" the secretary exclaimed, sitting on it. "It's as hard as stone, and there is barely a blanket to keep warm!"

Ram Dass held up his notepad. There, on the bottom of one of the pages, in big bold letters, he had written, "COMFORTABLE BED; WARM SILK BEDSPREAD."

"Do you really think we can give her everything she has pretended?" the secretary asked.

"We will give her more than even she could ever imagine," Ram Dass replied. "Mr. Carrisford has agreed to fund the secret operation. He has been making himself so sick over the missing Crewe girl that he will gladly do whatever he can to help this girl in the meantime."

Ram Dass smiled, remembering the gleam of hope that had come back into his kind employer's eyes when talking about the plan. "It will be good for him," he concluded.

"But do you really think it can be done while she sleeps?" the secretary asked.

"I can walk as softly as if my feet were made of

velvet," Ram Dass assured him. "And children sleep soundly—even unhappy ones."

"When she wakes up," the secretary said, "she will think a magician has been in her chambers! Like a story from *Arabian Nights*!"

Ram Dass agreed. After taking a few more notes, the two men slipped back out through the window as quietly as they had come in.

Melchisedec was very relieved. After he was sure the two strange men were gone, he came out of his hole again. He scuffled around a bit, in the hope that even the two scary strangers might have dropped a crumb or two.

CHAPTER 9

What Would a Princess Do?

The winter days grew shorter and so chilly that Sara became stiffer and more tired every day.

Becky was faring no better.

"If it weren't fer you, miss," she said one morning, before they began their day, "the prisoner in the next cell, I think I should die."

And with that, the girls set off downstairs, to do their drudge work.

Sara had to accomplish many things that day. And because the cook had been in an awful mood that morning, it seemed she would have to do them on an empty stomach.

The streets were soaked in a damp, cold mist, and Sara's raggedy clothes were quickly wet right through to the skin. The icy cold water went squish in her holey shoes, and the wind seemed to cut like a knife through her outgrown, flimsy jacket.

"Oh Becky," she thought, "perhaps I might die today as well."

Suddenly, Sara saw a shiny object just beneath her feet, in the muddy gutter. Bending down to take a closer look, she saw that it was really a few coins. They had probably fallen out of a hole in someone's pocket. She scooped them up with her cold, reddened hands.

"Oh," she gasped, "it is true!"

Just down the street was a bakery, in which a cheerful, stout woman was putting a tray of delicious, newly baked hot buns in a lit-up window.

More than anything, Sara wanted to take the coins and buy some fresh buns. Doing some math in her head, she might be able to pay for as many as four.

But then she frowned. She felt that it was wrong to use money that someone else had lost and might need. She looked around for someone to ask about the money, but there was nobody. And so she decided that she would at least ask the woman in the bakery if she had lost it.

The woman looked at Sara strangely.

"Bless us! No," she answered. "Did you find it?"

"Yes," Sara said, "in the gutter."

"Well then, keep it," said the woman. "It's a busy street. You'll never find out who lost it."

"I know," Sara said, "but I thought I would just ask you."

"Not many would," the woman said, looking at Sara with respect. "Do you want to buy something?"

"Yes, thank you," Sara said. "Four buns, if you please."

The woman could see that Sara was staring at the buns with hunger, as though she could eat one hundred in one big bite. So she kindly put six buns in the bag instead of four.

"Oh," Sara said, looking into the bag and noticing the mistake. "I said four, if you please. I can only pay for four."

"I threw in two for free," the woman said. "A baker's half dozen. I daresay you will be able to eat them all. Aren't you hungry?"

A mist rose before Sara's eyes. "I *am* very hungry. Thank you so much!"

On her way out of the bakery, however, something—or rather, someone—stopped Sara in her tracks. It was a little figure more pitiful even than herself—a figure that was not much more than a bundle of rags, from which small, bare, muddy red feet peeped out, because her rags were not long enough to cover them. Above the rags, Sara could see a dirty face with big, saucer-like, hungry eyes and a head of tangled hair that made her look like a wild animal.

"This girl," Sara thought, "is even worse off than I am."

As Sara came near, the little girl turned her head away, as though Sara was going to yell at her or shoo her out of the way, like everyone else did.

"Are you hungry?" Sara asked.

The little girl looked up in surprise.

"I am," she said. She told Sara that she had not eaten in days.

Sara couldn't believe she was going to do what she was about to do. "But after all," she thought, "what would a princess do?"

She reached into her bag, took out one of the buns, and gave it to the other little girl. The girl sat up straight, then grabbed it and crammed it into her mouth in one big, wolfish bite.

"Oh my," Sara heard her say in wild delight. "Oh my! Oh my!"

With shaking hands, Sara took out three more buns and handed them over, only to watch them be devoured in the same way.

She thought she might faint when she handed over the fifth bun. But, tightly clutching her one last bun, Sara managed to be strong enough to turn and walk away.

The little London beggar behind her was still gobbling up the buns. She was too intent on eating to thank Sara, but Sara didn't mind.

Meanwhile, from the bakery window, the woman couldn't believe her eyes.

"Why, I never!" she exclaimed. "That young woman gave her buns to a beggar child! And not because she wasn't starving herself, either—I could see that much in her eyes."

She opened the door to her shop and called down to the little beggar child to come up.

"Did that young woman give you her buns?" she asked her in the shop.

The beggar child nodded.

"How many?"

"Five," the child said.

The woman looked back at the road where Sara had been standing, feeling very heartsick.

"I wish she hadn't disappeared so quickly," she said. "If only I had given her a dozen buns!"

She turned to the beggar child who was still standing before her.

"Are you still hungry?" she said.

"Like always," was the answer.

"Well, come on in and warm yourself," the

woman said. Although a poor working woman herself, she offered to help the girl, out of pity for Sara. "Whenever you are cold and hungry, you can come inside, you hear? It's the least I can do for that young girl's sake."

Almost back at the school, her cold bun clutched tightly in her hand, Sara paused for a second before the Large house. The front door was open, and suitcases were being carried out. Someone was going on a journey.

Mr. Large kissed his wife in the doorway and then walked down the stairs to his waiting carriage.

"Will Moscow be covered with snow?" one of his children called after him. "Will you meet the Czar?"

"I will write and tell you all about it," Mr. Large called back, with a good-natured laugh. "Good night, duckies! God bless you!"

At that moment, Guy Clarence appeared in

the doorway. “If you find the little girl,” he shouted, “give her our love!”

Mr. Large got into his carriage, and the front door closed.

“I wonder who the little girl is,” Sara thought, “that he is going to look for so earnestly.”

And then, lugging her heavy basket, she, too, went inside and shut the door.

She, of course, had no clue that *she* was the mystery “who”—the little lost daughter of Captain Crewe.

CHAPTER 10

The Grand Feast

When Sara came home that evening, she was all tired out. Miss Minchin had yelled at her for returning home late from her errands. She didn't seem to care that the streets were wet and muddy, and that it had been hard for Sara to walk quickly in her worn-out shoes. The cook was in a bad mood, too, and took it out on Sara.

"May I have something to eat?" Sara asked shyly, laying the cook's purchases on the table.

"Dinner is over and done with," the cook snapped back at her as usual.

"Please," Sara said. "I am *so* hungry." She kept her voice low because she was afraid it would begin to shake.

"There's some bread in the pantry," the cook said. "And that's all you get."

Even though the bread was old, hard, and dry, Sara ate up every bite. "I'm sorry, Melchisedec," she thought, "but I won't have even one crumb left over for you tonight!"

It was always hard for her to climb the three long flights of stairs leading to the attic, but tonight she was so very tired, it seemed as though the stairs would never end. Several times, she had to stop and rest.

When she at last reached the top steps, she saw a glimmer of light coming from under her door. Ermengarde, she thought.

She was not in the mood for company. But she told herself that, if she lived in a castle, and

Ermengarde was the lady of another castle coming to visit, when she heard the sound of horns beyond the drawbridge she wouldn't be grumpy and say, "Please, tonight is not a good time." No, she would go down to receive her. Then she would lay a feast in the banquet room, and call in minstrels to sing and tell stories . . .

Well, there was no feast, and no minstrels singing and playing, but Princess Sara was ready to greet Ermengarde when she opened the door. Used to Melchisedec, but still slightly afraid, Ermengarde was sitting in the center of the bed where he would not be able to jump on her.

"Miss Amelia has gone out to spend the night with her old aunt," Ermengarde whispered. "No one else ever checks on us at night, so I could stay here until morning if I wanted to!"

Sara thought, "But *why* would you want to?"

"Oh Sara, you look so tired," Ermengarde said. "Tired and pale."

"I am tired," Sara said, plopping down onto the lopsided footstool.

"At least you are skinny," Ermengarde said with envy.

Sara felt like shaking Ermengarde and telling her that, if she were being starved by Miss Minchin, she would be skinny, too. But she bit her tongue. "I was always a thin child," she answered bravely.

Just then, both girls heard a ruckus on the stairs below. It was Miss Minchin's angry voice, scolding Becky.

"Will she come in here?" Ermengarde whispered, panic-stricken.

"I don't think so," Sara said, "but just in case, don't make a sound!"

Miss Minchin, after all, seldom climbed the last flight of stairs. She seemed to be doing it now, however, and dragging up Becky with her.

"You lying thief!" they heard her say. "Cook tells me that things have been taken from the kitchen on a regular basis!"

"It weren't me, mum," they heard Becky sob in reply. "I was hungry enough, but it weren't me—never!"

"Stop telling falsehoods. I should call the police and have you sent to prison! Half a meat pie indeed!" Miss Minchin pronounced.

Both Sara and Ermengarde heard a slap. They knew that Becky's ears had been boxed. Then they heard Becky's door shut and Miss Minchin start back down the stairs. Becky was crying softly into her pillow.

Sara started to shake. "That horrible cook!" she cried. "She takes things herself and blames Becky—Becky, who is so hungry she eats crusts out of the garbage can!" Sara pressed her hands to her face and burst into heartfelt little sobs.

Ermengarde stared at her friend with wide eyes. Slowly a thought made its way into her sluggish mind. "Sara," she said timidly, "I don't want to be rude, but are *you* ever hungry?"

This was too much for Sara. She blurted out, "What do you think, Ermengarde? Yes, I am hungry. I am so hungry I could almost eat you!"

Ermengarde drew in a breath. "I feel so stupid," she said, "but I never knew."

"I didn't want you to know," Sara said, laughing even as she kept crying. "It would have made me feel like a beggar."

"Sara!" Ermengarde cried out, giving an excited little jump. The ideas were starting to come faster now, and this was a good one. "This very afternoon, my aunt sent me a box full of treats. It's got cake in it, and meat pies, and jam tarts and buns, and oranges and red-currant cider, and figs and chocolate, and—"

"Stop it!" Sara said. Her head was spinning.

"I'll sneak back to my room and bring it upstairs and we can eat it, okay?"

"Oh Ermie," Sara said. "The magic always comes through, doesn't it? Just when you think that you can't go on, and that life is too awful, something nice happens. The worst never *quite* comes. We can pretend it is a dinner party! And oh, can I invite the prisoner in the next cell?"

Ermengarde agreed. While Ermengarde was gone, Sara knocked a coded invitation on the wall. Waiting for her to return, Sara looked around the attic with new and excited eyes.

"I need your help, Becky," she said, "to set the table for a grand feast!"

Finding Ermengarde's red shawl lying on the floor where it had been dropped, Sara threw it across an old table. Voilà—it was an elegant dining room sideboard covered with a rich red cloth. In her old chest, which was being stored up in her room, Sara found several old white handkerchiefs and arranged them on the tablecloth. They formed imaginary golden plates and dainty lace napkins.

Also among her old things, Becky found a summer hat trimmed with a wreath of faded flowers. Sara arranged these on the table as well to make a fine centerpiece. "Aren't their colors just glorious?" Sara asked. "Have you ever smelled such lovely perfume?"

At that moment, Ermengarde burst into the room, breathless from carrying her picnic hamper all the way up the stairs. "Why, it's a fancy banquet hall!" she said, upon seeing the table set. Sara smiled. Ermengarde had not forgotten her lessons on how to pretend.

"It's like a queen's table," sighed Becky.

"You be the princess and sit at the head of the table," Ermengarde told Sara.

However, the girls barely had time to be seated or to take one piece of cake into their hands when all three of them froze. It was the sound of someone climbing angrily and with a solemn purpose up the stairs. There was no mistake about who it was.

Miss Minchin struck open the door with a blow of her hand. Three frightened faces looked up at her.

"I had been suspecting this sort of thing," she said, "but I did not dream of such an affront. Lavinia was telling me the truth!"

Ermengarde burst into tears. "Please don't punish Sara or Becky," she begged. "It is my fault. My aunt sent me the box. We were only having a party—"

"With Princess Sara at the head of the table, I see," Miss Minchin said. "I'm sure this is *your* doing, Sara. Ermengarde isn't smart enough to have thought of such a thing."

Miss Minchin turned and stared at the banquet table, which, under her gaze, became sad and

pitiful once more. "You arranged all of this rubbish, no doubt."

When Sara nodded yes, Miss Minchin raised her arm. With a mean flourish, she swept the plates and flowers into Ermengarde's picnic hamper. "You will have no breakfast, lunch, or dinner tomorrow," she informed Sara.

"But I haven't had any lunch or dinner today," Sara replied, rather faintly.

"All the better," Miss Minchin replied.

She turned to Ermengarde. "Really, Ermengarde. What would your papa say if he knew where you were tonight?"

As Miss Minchin was preparing to leave, something in Sara's face caught her eye. It was that same look that always maddened her. Tonight it seemed irksome indeed.

"Why are you looking at me like that?" she asked. "What are you thinking about now?"

"I was just wondering," Sara said, "what *my*

papa would say if he knew where I was tonight."

"How dare you, you brazen child!" Miss Minchin had lost her temper once again. "I will leave you to wonder," she said. And, shoving the hamper into Ermengarde's arms, she dragged her out by the scruff of the neck. Sara was left standing all alone in the dark.

All alone, that is, except for the dark face of Ram Dass, who was watching in anger from the roof outside of Sara's window. He had walked across because he had heard the ruckus through the walls and wanted to make sure his little friend was all right.

She was not all right, he saw, as he watched Sara curl up on the bed and cry herself to sleep. But if he and Carrisford had anything to do with it, by tomorrow, perhaps, she would be better.

CHAPTER 11

The Magic

Sara did not know how long she had slept, but when she came to slowly the next morning, eyes still closed, she knew that she needed to sleep longer. Even Miss Minchin let her sleep an extra hour on Sundays.

Or perhaps she was still sleeping—dreaming, really. How else could she feel so warm and comfortable? When she put out her hand, how else could she feel covered by a warm quilt? How else could she hear the gentle crackling of a fire in her rusty old grate?

A bit later, she opened her eyes. And like a miracle, the dream continued. Along with all of the things she had pretended—the thick, soft blue Indian rug, the soft sofa with cushions to curl up on, and a tiger-skin rug in front of the fire—was a small folding table. It was covered with a white cloth, topped with a small, piping hot feast of savory soups, sandwiches, toast, and muffins.

How, she did not know, but somehow she was sleeping in a new bed, covered in warm, fluffy blankets. At the foot of the bed were a warm silk robe and a pair of quilted slippers. Best of all, in a pile by the chair near the fire were some lovely books.

Looking all around, she could see rose-colored lamps, wall hangings and pictures, colorful rugs and cushions, flowers in pretty vases, and any number of other wonderful, magical things.

"Why does it not melt away?" she panted. "Oh, I never had such a dream before!"

Springing out of bed, she ran around the room touching everything. She brought her hand as close as she could to the fire. "It's hot!" she cried, pulling back. She put on the robe and pressed the material to her cheek. "It's so warm and soft!" she cried. She tasted some of the lovely food that had been left for her on the table. "Delicious!" she cried. "And it's real, all of it! I am not dreaming!"

Suddenly, she saw a little note resting upon the pile of books. "To the little girl in the attic," the note said, "from a friend."

Reading those words, Sara did a strange thing. She put her face down on the page and burst into tears. "Somebody cares for me," she sobbed. "I do have a friend."

Imagine, if you can, what the rest of the morning was like. Right away, Sara knocked on the wall for Becky, and the two girls spent the next few hours sitting before the blazing fire. At first Becky was speechless from fear. But once Becky got over her own disbelief, they both gobbled up the food. Even more important, their hearts were fed by the magical kindness of Sara's secret friend. Somehow, their fear of Miss Minchin faded into the background. Sara decided that she would keep the wonders that had happened to them a secret, if such a thing were possible.

Soon, of course, they would have to go downstairs to work, but that day both girls did so with courage. They had extra color in their cheeks and spring in their steps.

Everyone at the school had heard about what happened the night before, so they all expected Sara to come down looking humbled and shamefaced. But instead, she seemed to float around looking even more regal than usual.

"She doesn't even look hungry," Lavinia whispered to Jessie. Lavinia knew about Sara's punishment and was not the least bit sorry to have told on her. "Perhaps she is just pretending she had a good breakfast!"

Miss Minchin sternly warned Sara, "Remember that you are in disgrace. It is rude of you to go around looking like you had just come into a fortune!"

The weather on this day was possibly even worse than it was the last time Sara had gone out to run errands—wetter, muddier, and colder. Her basket was heavier, and the cook was more testy. But somehow, today she could bear it all. Even if the magic was gone when she returned to her room that night, she thought, she would still always be grateful and know that it had saved her.

When she pushed open the door to her room that night, she gasped. She shut the door and, standing with her back to it, looked from side to side. Not only was the magic still there, but it had new life. A freshly built fire was blazing, even more merrily than before. More finery, pictures, and pillows filled the room. And best of all, a delicious dinner had been made, steamy hot, just waiting for her on the table. And all the dirty breakfast plates had been cleared away.

When Becky came in, she started giggling like someone who was out of her mind. The two girls sat down to dinner like two princesses.

From then on, every day Sara returned to her room, something new had been added. And when there was no more space left in Sara's room, the magic began to spill over into Becky's room. Sara said to herself, "Is this my attic room? And am I that same cold, raggedy, damp little girl? I must be living in a fairy story."

Everyone who was mean to the girls before was still mean, but it hardly mattered. The color came back into their fattening cheeks. Soon their eyes no longer seemed too big for their faces.

"Sara Crewe and Becky are looking so wonderfully well," Miss Amelia observed, speaking to her sister. "Before they were looking like little starvelings."

"Well, why shouldn't they!" Miss Minchin snapped, covering up for her own misdeeds. "They are treated kindly."

Sometimes, Sara thought that she might hide and catch her secret friend in the act. But that would ruin the magic. Still, she did want to thank her benefactor, and so she wrote him a note. She signed it, "The Little Girl in the Attic." The next morning, along with the dinner dishes, the note had disappeared.

CHAPTER 12

Lost and Found

One day, Sara and Becky were enjoying their secret morning treat when they heard a soft scratching at the window. The monkey's face appeared in the window. The next second, just as he had before, he lifted up the windowpane and climbed down into Sara's room.

When Becky shrieked, Sara said, "It's okay. He's just the sweet little monkey from next door. Doesn't he look like a little baby?"

"A very ugly little baby," Becky said, slowly

coming closer. "What are you going to do with him?"

"Well," Sara said, "I know that Ram Dass and the Indian gentleman will be quite wild with worry when they discover him missing. So I must take him back over immediately."

Next door, no one had yet noticed that the monkey was missing because Mr. Carmichael had just returned from Moscow, with bad news to report. He had been unable to find the little Crewe girl. Mr. Carrisford, who had been cheered up for a time by Ram Dass's secret mission next door, all at once turned completely weary and miserable.

"Come, come," Carmichael said, in his cheery voice. "We'll find her yet."

They were interrupted by an announcement of a visitor. Ram Dass told them that it was the child from next door bringing back the monkey, which had just broken into her attic room.

"I thought it might please you to see and to speak with her," Ram Dass suggested.

Mr. Carrisford quickly filled in Mr. Carmichael on the details of his and Ram Dass's magical plan to help the girl next door. The children squealed with delight.

Sara then made her entrance with a curtsy.

"Your monkey ran away again," she told the Indian gentleman in her pretty voice. "I thought you might be worried. Shall I give him to the *lascar*?"

"How do you know he is a *lascar*?" Nora asked with wonder.

"Oh, I know *lascars*," Sara said. "I was born in India."

The Indian gentleman sat bolt upright so suddenly that, for a moment, Sara was scared.

"Question her, Carmichael," he said. "I cannot."

The big, kind father of the Large Family knew

how to question little girls. And Sara liked to tell stories. So within a few minutes she had told all of hers. She explained everything: from her papa losing all of his money in the diamond mines because of a friend who let him down and then ran away, to being forced to work as a scullery maid at Miss Minchin's boarding school. Then she came to the final chapter—the magic that may have saved her life.

"What was your father's name?" the Indian gentleman said, his voice faint.

"Captain Ralph Crewe," Sara said proudly.

"Carmichael!" the invalid gasped. "It is the child!" For a moment, the ailing Carrisford seemed to faint dead away. Ram Dass had to rush out of the room for a bottle of smelling salts. He held them under Carrisford's nose to revive him.

"What child am I?" Sara asked timidly.

Mr. Carmichael spoke calmly, so as not to scare her.

"Mr. Carrisford was your father's friend. But he didn't betray your father or lose your father's money. He only *thought* he had, because he was so ill from brain fever. By the time he recovered, your poor papa was dead. Mr. Carrisford has been looking for you ever since. He has searched for you all over Europe—in France and Moscow—and here you were, all this time!"

"Yes—for two years, just on the other side of the wall," Sara finished. She could not believe how long she had waited. A thought flew into her head. "Wait a minute," she said. "Did Ram Dass bring the things across the roof and into my room?"

"Yes!" Janet answered. "Mr. Carrisford was your rich secret friend."

Sara threw her thin arms around the Indian gentleman and hugged him as hard as she could.

"This is exactly the medicine my friend needed," Carmichael thought happily.

Suddenly, Miss Minchin came rushing into the room, following by a maid begging everyone's pardon. One of the students had seen Sara enter the house next door.

Sara rose and became rather pale, but Mr. Carrisford put a steady hand upon her head to calm her.

"I am sorry to bother you," Miss Minchin said in a huff. "I am Miss Minchin, the headmistress of the young ladies' boarding school next door. And I am so sorry that this child has given you trouble." She turned to face Sara. "You—go home at once! You will be severely punished."

But the Indian gentleman held Sara at his side. "She is not going anywhere. She *is* home."

Miss Minchin drew back in amazement. "What could you possibly mean?" she gasped.

Mr. Carrisford wished to waste no more time with Miss Minchin.

And so, Mr. Carmichael related the whole

story. He told her that Carrisford was Captain Crewe's business partner in the diamond mines. He explained how the fortune that was thought to be lost was not only found, but found to have grown much larger.

Now it would all belong to Sara.

Miss Minchin, not being such a clever woman, was foolish enough to make one last attempt to lay claim to Sara's fortune.

"Captain Crewe left his daughter in my charge," Miss Minchin spoke. "I will not allow her to leave. The law will step in to help me. And if she stays here, I will be sure never to let her see any of her friends again!"

"The law will come to *Sara's* aid," Carrisford corrected her. "And I am sure that the parents of Miss Crewe's fellow pupils will not refuse her invitations to visit her at her new guardian's house."

Miss Minchin startled. She knew that Mr.

Carrisford was right. Who would refuse to let their children play with the future heiress to a large fortune? And so, curtsying clumsily and muttering to herself, she slunk away.

When she got home, Miss Amelia was waiting for her. Miss Amelia was mad.

"I've had it, sister," Amelia said, with a burst of courage. "I often thought that you were treating Sara poorly, but I never said anything. She was clever and good, and would have repaid you any kindness. But you didn't show her any, did you? You are a selfish, hard-hearted woman!"

"Why Amelia!" Miss Minchin gasped.

"Still," Amelia continued, "she always behaved herself like a little princess, no matter how awful we were to her. And now you've lost her. Some other school will get her, and her money. And the worst part is that she and her new guardian will tell everyone how we treated her. They will find out about her thin, shabby clothes, the scant food, and the hard work. If all our pupils were taken away and we lost everything, it would serve us right!"

Miss Minchin didn't know what to say. By her silence, she showed that she knew Miss Amelia was correct. And, truth be told, from that point on, Miss Minchin became a little afraid of her sister.

With Sara gone, it was Ermengarde's turn to be the storyteller. She knew all about what had happened from Sara's long letter to her.

"There were diamond mines," she informed the other girls, "with millions and millions of diamonds in each of them. And now, Sara will be more of a princess than she ever was! So there!"

Sara hadn't yet written to Becky. But Becky had overheard the other girls talking. Although she was happy for Sara, she feared that the magic in her own life would disappear with her.

As she climbed the final steps to Sara's old room, she paused. There would be no fire tonight, she thought, no rosy lamp, no supper, and no princess telling marvelous stories.

But she must face it, she thought. And so, choking down a sob, she pushed open the door.

She was right about one thing: there was no princess. But there was a rosy lamp, and supper, and a dark-faced gentleman in a white turban smiling at her.

"Becky," Ram Dass said, "Sara did not forget you. She told Mr. Carrisford everything. And he has asked you to come to him tomorrow. You are to be Miss Sara's personal assistant." He waved his hands at all of the wonderful things he had brought during the past weeks. "Tonight, I shall take these things back over the roof to my house."

With that, he bowed politely to her and slipped back through the skylight. His ease showed Becky how he must have done it before.

Oh, how happy the Large children were! The mere fact of Sara's hardships and adventures made her priceless. Everybody wanted to hear, again and again, about the things that had happened to her. Their favorite story was about the royal banquet and the dream that turned out to be true.

Sitting next to Sara by the fire, the Indian gentleman smiled. That was his favorite part of the story as well.

"I am so glad," Sara said. "I am so glad it was you who were my friend!"

And there never were such friends as those two became. It was not the same as having her papa back, but it was the next best thing. Sara and Mr. Carrisford seemed to suit each other in a wonderful way. Just like her father had, he delighted in giving her things and surprising her. Especially in light of the dreadful things that had

happened to her, he knew there was no danger of her ever becoming spoiled.

As though to prove his point, Sara boldly told him about a plan for which she needed his help.

"What is it, Princess?" he asked. "How can I help?"

Sara told him about the woman in the bakery and the hungry little beggar girl in the streets outside. "If I have so much money," she asked, "might I tell the woman that, on cold and dreadful days, she can feed all of the hungry beggar children and send the bills to me?"

"We shall arrange it tomorrow morning," agreed the Indian gentleman. He vowed to himself that, in reality, he would pay the bills.

The next morning, while Miss Minchin watched bitterly from the window, Sara climbed into the Large Family's carriage, wrapped in a new fur coat. That day, she carried out the first of her many plans to help others. The Little Missus had lived through much loss and sadness, but had come through it knowing that the world was still full of magic.

This was only the beginning, she realized, of a new and wonderful life.

What Do *You* Think?

Questions for Discussion

Have you ever been around a toddler who keeps asking the question "Why?" Does your teacher call on you in class with questions from your homework? Do your parents ask you questions at the dinner table about your day ? We are always surrounded by questions that need a specific response. But is it possible to have a question with no right answer?

The following questions are about the book you just read. But this is not a quiz! They are designed to help you look at the people, places, and events in the story from different angles. These questions do not have specific answers. Instead, they might make you think of the story in a completely new way.

Think carefully about each question and enjoy discovering more about this classic story.

1. Sara tells her father, “If I have plenty of books, I guess I shall be all right.” Why does she say this? Do you have any books that make you feel that way? Which ones and why?

2. Sara is a very imaginative child. She believes that her doll, Emily, can hear her speaking and comes to life when no one is around. Do you believe that toys lead secret lives? Do you have a specific toy that you confide in?

3. Sara likes to pretend that she is a princess. Why has she chosen this particular fantasy? What do you like to pretend to be?

4. Neither Sara nor Lottie has a mother. In what ways has this shaped their personalities?

How do the two girls compare with orphan characters you have read about in other books?

5. Miss Minchin feels uneasy about Sara because "the little girl almost seemed to see right through her." What do you think this means? Have you ever felt that way about someone?

6. Mariette calls Sara a "perfect little princess." Is she paying Sara a compliment or is she teasing her?

7. No one seemed to take any notice of Sara after Miss Minchin made her a maid in the school. In fact, most of the girls seemed to deliberately avoid her. Why do you think this happened? Have you ever experienced something similar with your friends?

8. When Ermengarde finally admits Sara that she misses her best friend, Sara confesses that she misses Ermengarde, too, but was too proud to say anything first. Have you ever been in a similar situation with your best friend? How did it turn out?

9. After finding some coins on the street, Sara buys four buns for herself, but then gives them to a beggar girl. Why does she do this? Have you ever given away something that you wanted for yourself? What was it?

10. Sara says that "everything is a story!" Do you believe this statement is true? If so, how could you show that everything in your life is a story?

Afterword

by Arthur Pober, EdD

First impressions are important.

Whether we are meeting new people, going to new places, or picking up a book unknown to us, first impressions count for a lot. They can lead to warm, lasting memories or can make us shy away from any future encounters.

Can you recall your own first impressions and earliest memories of reading the classics?

Do you remember wading through pages and pages of text to prepare for an exam? Or were you the child who hid under the blanket to read with a flashlight, joining forces with Robin Hood to save Maid Marian? Do you remember only how long it took you to read a lengthy novel such as *Little Women*? Or did you become best friends with the March sisters?

Even for a gifted young reader, getting through long chapters with dense language can easily become overwhelming and can obscure the richness of the story and its characters. Reading an abridged, newly crafted version of a classic novel can be the gentle introduction a child needs to explore the characters and story line without the frustration of difficult vocabulary and complex themes.

Reading an abridged version of a classic novel gives the young reader a sense of independence and the satisfaction of finishing a "grown-up" book. And when a child is engaged with and inspired by a classic story, the tone is set for further exploration of the story's themes, characters, history, and details. As a child's reading skills advance, the desire to tackle the original, unabridged version of the story will naturally emerge.

If made accessible to young readers, these stories can become invaluable tools for understanding themselves in the context of their families and social environments. This is why the Classic Starts series includes questions that stimulate discussion regarding the impact and social relevance of the characters and stories today. These questions can foster lively conversations between children and their parents or teachers. When we look at the issues, values, and standards of past times in terms of how we live now, we can appreciate literature's classic tales in a very personal and engaging way.

Share your love of reading the classics with a young child, and introduce an imaginary world real enough to last a lifetime.

Dr. Arthur Pober, EdD

Dr. Arthur Pober has spent more than twenty years in the fields of early-childhood and gifted education. He is the former principal of one of the world's oldest laboratory schools for gifted youngsters, Hunter College Elementary School, and former director of Magnet Schools for the Gifted and Talented for more than 25,000 youngsters in New York City.

Dr. Pober is a recognized authority in the areas of media and child protection and is currently the U.S. representative to the European Institute for the Media and European Advertising Standards Alliance.

Explore these wonderful stories in our Classic Starts® library.

20,000 Leagues Under the Sea
The Adventures of Huckleberry Finn
The Adventures of Robin Hood
The Adventures of Sherlock Holmes
The Adventures of Tom Sawyer
Alice in Wonderland & Through the Looking-Glass
Animal Stories
Anne of Avonlea
Anne of Green Gables
Arabian Nights
Around the World in 80 Days
Ballet Stories
Black Beauty
The Call of the Wild
Dracula
Five Little Peppers and How They Grew
Frankenstein
Great Expectations
Greek Myths
Grimm's Fairy Tales
Gulliver's Travels
Heidi
The Hunchback of Notre-Dame
The Iliad
Journey to the Center of the Earth
The Jungle Book

The Last of the Mohicans

Little Lord Fauntleroy

Little Men

A Little Princess

Little Women

The Man in the Iron Mask

Moby-Dick

The Odyssey

Oliver Twist

Peter Pan

The Phantom of the Opera

Pinocchio

Pollyanna

The Prince and the Pauper

Rebecca of Sunnybrook Farm

The Red Badge of Courage

Robinson Crusoe

Roman Myths

The Secret Garden

The Story of King Arthur and His Knights

The Strange Case of Dr. Jekyll and Mr. Hyde

The Swiss Family Robinson

The Three Musketeers

The Time Machine

Treasure Island

The Voyages of Doctor Dolittle

The War of the Worlds

White Fang

The Wind in the Willows